PiZAZZ

VS. THE NEW KID

PiZAZZ

VS. THE NEW KID

Sophy Henn

ALADDIN

New York   London   Toronto   Sydney   New Delhi

ALADDIN

An imprint of Simon & Schuster Children's Publishing Division
1230 Avenue of the Americas, New York, New York 10020
First Aladdin hardcover edition June 2021
Copyright © 2020 by Sophy Henn. All rights reserved.
Originally published in Great Britain in 2020 by Simon & Schuster UK Ltd.
Also available in an Aladdin paperback edition.
All rights reserved, including the right of reproduction in whole or in part in any form.
ALADDIN and related logo are registered trademarks of Simon & Schuster, Inc.
For information about special discounts for bulk purchases, please contact Simon & Schuster
Special Sales at 1-866-506-1949 or business@simonandschuster.com.
The Simon & Schuster Speakers Bureau can bring authors to your live event.
For more information or to book an event contact the Simon & Schuster Speakers Bureau at
1-866-248-3049 or visit our website at www.simonspeakers.com.
The illustrations for this book were rendered digitally.
The text of this book was set in New Clarendon MT.
Manufactured in the United States of America 0421 FFG
2 4 6 8 10 9 7 5 3 1
This book has been cataloged with the Library of Congress.
ISBN 978-1-5344-9246-2 (hc)
ISBN 978-1-5344-9245-5 (pbk)
ISBN 978-1-5344-9247-9 (eBook)

MEET THE SUPERS ...

my mum

my dad

AKA ATOMIC

AKA ORB

my ANNOYING little sister

AKA RED

DRAGON

Wanda

½ dog ½ telephone

randma
AKA RAY
Gramps
AKA INFERNO
AUNTY BLAZE
SHE'S SO COOOOOOL
Uncle Titano-ooooo
Teaser
Granny
my secret baddie friend
UH-OH
Aunty FURY
APOW

The bit where I tell you the story so far . . .

SO . . .

Well, I am still 9¼, very nearly 9½, and I am still a **SUPERHERO**, and unfortunately my name is still **PIZAZZ**. Apparently I am absolutely NOT allowed to change it. **EYE ROLL**

You probably think being a **SUPERHERO** is pretty cool, but when your whole family are **SUPERHEROES**, it doesn't feel very cool. I mean, my **mum** and **dad** are about the furthest from cool you can get, and **Grandma** and **Gramps** are lovely, but cool? I don't think so.

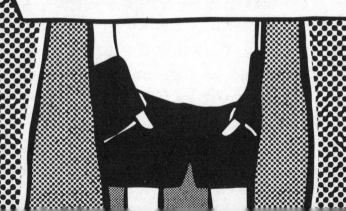

AND THEN THERE'S . . .

RED DRAGON AKA the Most Annoying Little Sister EVER, who only gets high grades and is the head of the student council and volunteers to teach the little kids to read and makes perfect cakes and is basically good at **EVERYTHING . . . BUT** I can burp the alphabet. So who is the real winner here?

Yep. . . . It's her.

If that wasn't bad enough, I get bossed about by our pet dog. Meet **WANDA**.

She came to us from **Mission Control**. Basically she receives messages about **top secret** *SUPERHERO* missions, then she bosses us off to deal with them.

side-eye

Oh yes,
and then
there is . . . .

EVERYTHING ELSE!

*SUPER*powers are cool, unless you are me and have the **MOST** embarrassing *SUPER*power in the whole universe.

Then I am always having to dash off to save the planet. And always at the **WORST** possible moment. **UGH.**

AND guess what? I have to wear a stupid *SUPERHERO* costume the whole time.

So now you know. Being a *SUPERHERO* isn't as good as you probably think it is. And I am stuck with it **FOREVER** . . .

. . . *SUPER*.

EYE ROLL

2

The bit about
the new kid

AWESOME SPACE ACADEMY

Even though I am a **SUPERHERO**, who saves the world more often than she is allowed ice cream, I still have to go to school. And not some sort of awesome **space academy superhero school** with hoverboards and neon lighting and teachers with *LASER EYES*. I have to go to normal school, with

normal kids who have normal names and normal clothes. So I blend in perfectly.

Well, not **everyone** is completely normal. I mean, there is Susan Briggs, and she can dislocate her thumbs just like that. And then there's Freddie Hayes, who can eat fifteen strawberry yogurts in a single lunchtime, and also Mr. Jones, the PE teacher—he is definitely **not normal**. . . .

And I suppose **Serena** and **The Populars** aren't exactly normal. I mean, they are in lots of ways because they don't have anything even slightly unusual about them. But somehow, by being **EXTREMELY** normal, they are **SUPER** popular and everyone wants to impress them. And even then **Serena** always looks like she has just smelled something very unpleasant, like **DABOMB'S STINK-BOMB STINK** (which of course she hasn't because I deal with that so she doesn't have to).

Plus **Serena** manages to look really bored at the same time. It's like she's thinking, "Ugh! What's that smell? It's REALLY disgusting but also REALLY boring." I am actually **secretly** impressed by it.

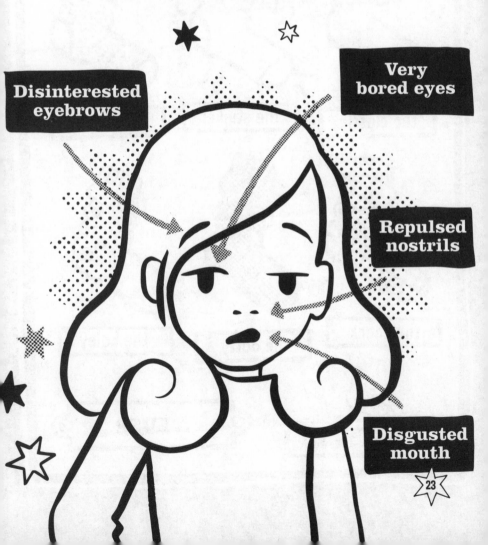

Disinterested eyebrows

Very bored eyes

Repulsed nostrils

Disgusted mouth

BEST SLOUCHY SOCK COLLECTION . . .

the classic

the stinker

the stripey

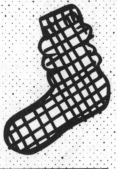

the check

the dotty

the holey

the shrunk-in-the-wash

. . . EVER

My friend Ivy and I both said that while it might be nice to be popular and have everyone practically worship you and be able to do anything you wanted and have the **best collection of slouchy socks EVER**, there is no way we would be as snooty and mean as Serena is. Ivy and I said you would have thought that being **super popular** for doing almost nothing would make you happy and nice, but no. And Serena absolutely never ever does anything for anyone else or uses her popular powers for good. Ivy and I said we totally would. If we were popular. Which we aren't.

Well, Ivy said all that and I agreed. **Strongly.**

Anyway, ever since I stopped Serena's dad, Mr. Piffle, from bulldozing the park next to school by using my **jazz hands/glitter storm** superpower move (SOOOOOO embarrassing), she has had it in for me more than **EVER**.

WRITING

BREATHING

EYE ROLL

HA HA HA

EYE ROLL

27

. . . I am not exactly thrilled at all that laughing at me, I try to distract myself by thinking about far more interesting things like **doughnuts**, my new hobby of putting googly eyes on EVERYTHING, and the rumor that is all over school about a **NEW KID** starting in MY YEAR. This is actually quite exciting for lots of reasons. . . .

I will no longer be the **NEW KID**. **HOORAY!** I mean, technically both me and my sister, **RED**, were **NEW KIDS** together about five months ago when our parents made us move here so we could be nearer **Gramps** and **Grandma**. But OBVIOUSLY **RED** fit in right away, so being "the **NEW KID**" was left to me.

 They could be less cool than me and might make me look a bit cooler.

 They might like me. I mean, they MIGHT.

 They might bring **doughnuts**. Which, thinking about it, is exactly what I should have done when I started.

I mean, who doesn't like the person with the **doughnuts**?

THE ECO COUNCIL

I had a lunchtime meeting with my best friends Ivy, **Ed**, and **Molly**, otherwise known as the **ECO COUNCIL** because guess what? I save the planet when I am at school as well as the rest of the time. **I KNOW!** It's just nonstop! We were discussing how on earth we could sort out a compost area for the school cafeteria food waste when **Molly** said she had some exciting news that wasn't **ECO-COUNCIL** related, and if she didn't tell us she would burst. We took a vote and unanimously agreed that none of us wanted **Molly** to burst, so then she told us that her mum's sister's husband's best friend's brother does house-decorating, AND that he was decorating a house nearby AND that the house happened to belong to a certain **NEW KID** and their family. Then she said we would NEVER guess what?

Well, we all tried to guess.

I guessed they ran a **doughnut** shop. Ivy guessed the entire family were all published novelists. And **Ed** guessed that they were a family band and each member played a different brass instrument.

Amazingly, none of us were right. So **Molly** told us . . .

. . . the new family were all

SUPERS!!

3

Even though we had all sworn on Ivy's lucky pen to keep this news **top secret**, SOME-HOW it had sneaked out (**Ed**, definitely **Ed**—he is the **WORST** with secrets), and by the end of school everyone knew that a new *SUPER* was coming.

As we walked home, I told Ivy I wasn't at all sure how I felt about this. While I definitely hated being the only *SUPER* in school (as I said, my *SUPER*-annoying sister who fit in perfectly in NO seconds doesn't count), I wasn't at all sure what it would be like to have another one in school. As in, what would it be like for ME? I decided I needed to have a really good think about this and was just wondering what color to paint my nails because painting my nails helps me think (current favorite color . . . **Slimelight**). But then I stopped thinking quite suddenly because my face landed on the ground. After a second of feeling very confused, I realized I had *tripped*. This sort of thing seems to happen to me a lot, and I think it all stems from the time I was hit on the head by a **LLAMA** (long story). Of course, **Serena** and **The Populars** were all there to see this and kindly showed their concern by laughing hysterically.

EYE ROLL

And when I looked to see what I had actually tripped over, it turned out to be **WANDA**. . . .

THE SUPERS ARRIVE...WITH MUM'S LAST-MINUTE SHOPPING...

YUM!

BUT THE BAGS ARE PACKED FULL OF UNHEALTHY SNACKS...WHICH OUR TEAM START TO THROW INTO THE GUZZLER'S *GINORMOUS* MOUTH!

MUNCH MUNCH YUM! MUM! MUNCH MUNCH MUNCH

YUM! YUM!

MORE SNACKS? SURELY NOT...THIS ISN'T LIKE MUM...

GROAN GROAN

AND THEN THE *GUZZLER* SUDDENLY LOST HIS APPETITE AFTER FILLING UP ON TOO MANY SNACKS AND THE TOWN WAS SAFE FOR ANOTHER DAY.

THANKS, PIZAZZ AND RED! I JUST DID TO THE GUZZLER WHAT YOU GUYS DO *ALL* THE TIME!

When we got home, **Dad** cooked spaghetti with **eXTRA CHiLi,** which was surprising to literally no one because, while he makes it sound fancy by saying it's his **signature dish**, we all know it's the only thing he can actually cook. So that left no time for thinking . . . just dinner and homework.

I was super tired after dinner, but still a bit bothered about the **NEW KID**, so I went and got BERNARD from her (yes, **HER**) cage and sneaked her upstairs so we could talk it all over. She is actually a very good listener for a guinea pig. This might be because she can't talk back, but I really honestly think she

understands what I'm saying, even if it looks like she's just eating my schoolbooks.

I told **BERNARD** about the **NEW KID** and how they were **SUPER** too and how they would be in my year at school, and how I wasn't sure I liked having another **SUPER** in my school and how this was **VERY** confusing as I also didn't like being the only **SUPER** in my school, but maybe that was because I just didn't like being a **SUPER** at all, which was partly because of **Serena** picking on me, which was mainly because of me being **SUPER**. . . . And then I stopped talking to **BERNARD**, partly because that was possibly the longest sentence I had ever said and I was a bit out of breath, but also because I realized right then that I had to make friends with the **NEW KID** so I could save them from being picked on by **Serena**, just like I had been. And still was.

I KNOW! I just can't stop saving things.

It was **extremely hard** to get out of bed the next morning on account of staying up late and chatting to a guinea pig, so I got ready in a bit of a rush. (Actually, it was a personal best of six minutes and forty-two seconds—thanks.) When I eventually got to class and everyone seemed to be staring at me more than they usually do, I had a bit of a **panic**, so I went through my checklist. . . .

Clothes ☑

No breakfast on face ☑

Cape NOT tucked ☑
into underpants

So what was wrong with everyone? Ivy came over as soon as she saw me, with a face that sort of looked worried and **really, really happy** all at the same time.

Ivy told me that the **NEW KID** was starting today, and then her face just looked worried, so I told her about my chat with BERNARD and how I had realized that actually we should definitely make friends with the **NEW KID**, because if anyone knew what it was like to be *SUPER* around here, it was me. And then

Ivy looked just happy and told me that was a relief as the **NEW KID** was going to be in **OUR CLASS**. Well, this was FANTASTIC NEWS. Not so much for the **NEW KID**, as they would be right under **Serena's** slightly upturned nose, but great for me as I could be their "buddy" and look after them. Like **Mrs. Harris** had made **Serena** look after me when I started. Except I would actually look after them and not try to lose them around school.

The bell rang and **Mrs. Harris** rushed into class with a yellow flash trailing behind her. The yellow flash turned out to be the **NEW KID**, who stood at the front of the class looking like she wanted to be beamed up anywhere, even onto a **gunk-o-tron alien spaceship**, and we all know how disgusting **THAT** can be. **REALLY *DISGUSTING***. And quite **GUNKY**.

I remembered my first day when I was standing up there nervous, in front of the whole class, and I actually felt quite excited that I could help the **NEW KID** with settling in and everything. I looked over to see what **Serena** was doing, but it was like she hadn't even noticed the **NEW KID**. I am not sure even *her* nails are **THAT** distracting. Then **Mrs. Harris** took attendance and then she dropped her planner and then she picked it up and then she picked up all the tiny pieces of paper that had dropped out of her planner and then **FINALLY** she got around to the yellow flash.

The **NEW KID** was in actual fact called **JETT**, and she had moved here from another school. Then Mrs. Harris told us that **JETT** was a **SUPER**, which we all knew anyway because:

 Molly's mum's sister's husband's best friend's brother told **Molly** and then she told us and then **Ed** told EVERYONE.

 She was wearing a capelet (why couldn't I have one of those? You would have to try extremely hard to trip over that) and a **SUPERHERO** eye mask and everything she was wearing was YELLOW. Really, really, REALLY yellow.

 She was hovering a foot above the ground.

Then **Mrs. Harris** asked for a volunteer to be **JETT'S** "**BUDDY**," and I put my hand straight up and was feeling very good about myself as a nice, kind, and thoughtful person, ready to take this **NEW KID** under my wing and show her the ropes and make sure she didn't suffer the same humiliation I had and then . . .

I heard **Serena** say she wanted to do it, and **Mrs. Harris** say, "Okay, **JETT**, who do you pick to be your **BUDDY**?"

And

JETT

picked

Serena.

And then I thought . . .

WHAT?

REALLY?

YES.

REALLY.

I was surprised at how disappointed I felt. I mean, I didn't even know **JETT**, but then I tried to feel pleased for her as she had had two people volunteer to be her buddy, and one of them was the most popular person in school.

But unfortunately, I couldn't concentrate on that as I kept wondering how come **Serena** actually WANTED to hang out with **JETT**? And how come **JETT** hadn't picked me to be her buddy—I mean, what's wrong with me? And how come she had a short practical capelet that probably never got soggy because it never dragged in puddles, and not a **STUPID LONG CAPE** that always did?

OH, AND . . .

HOW COME EVERYTHING'S SO COMPLETELY UNFAIR???

4

The bit where I try to do the right thing . . .

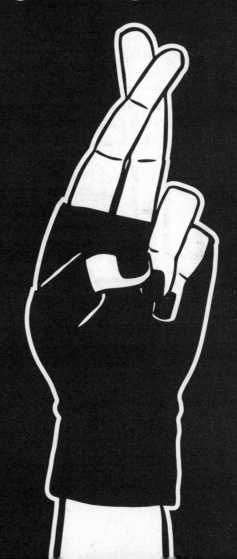

When I got home, **Dad** was making spaghetti with **EVEN MORE CHiLi**, **AGAIN**, RED was busy baking a cake for her next student council meeting EYE ROLL, and **Mum** was fixing the washing machine

(so far, so boring), **BUT**, brilliantly, Aunty Blaze had popped by with Uncle Titanoooooo. (Yes, there are that many o's.)

They had just been sorting out a squabble in the outer reaches of the galaxy and had been passing by, so they stopped in. It's really exciting when they come over; they are so snazzy and whizzy and always having **REALLY** exciting adventures. **Mum** said she and **Dad** used to be like that too, before they had me and **RED**, but I just can't see it myself.

Anyway, **Aunty Blaze** and Uncle Titanooooo asked me how my day was, and I told them all about **JETT** and how **Serena** had actually volunteered to be her buddy, which might seem like a nice thing to do, but this was **Serena** and she didn't really do "nice." And, anyway, I would have made a much better buddy, but **JETT** had picked **Serena**, and I was trying not to feel upset about it. But I did a bit.

Then **Aunty Blaze** told me why **JETT** had moved to our town— she knows stuff like that as she has a super-important job at **Mission Control**.

AUNTY BLAZE EXPLAINED THAT...

...JETT WAS PICKED ON AT HER OLD SCHOOL BECAUSE SHE WAS A SUPER. APPARENTLY HAVING A CAPELET, BEING ABLE TO FLY, AND CONSTANTLY DASHING OFF TO SAVE THE WORLD MADE HER STAND OUT, AND SO SOME OF THE OTHER KIDS HAD TEASED HER.

SO I SAID...

HUH! *REALLY?* I WOULD NEVER HAVE GUESSED THAT, AS THAT SORT OF THING *NEVER* HAPPENS TO ME. EXCEPT FOR *EVERY SINGLE DAY.*

AND AUNTY BLAZE SAID...

WELL, IN THAT CASE *I* WOULD COMPLETELY UNDERSTAND WHY JETT MIGHT WANT TO JUST BLEND IN A BIT AND NOT DRAW ATTENTION TO HER SUPERNESS, HMMMMMMMM?

I said I guessed that explained why JETT might not pick me as her buddy, but now she had picked Serena, who is actually the person most likely to pick on anyone for anything! Uncle Titanoooooo told me that SUPERS look out for one another, no matter what, and as a fellow SUPER I had to try to keep an eye out for JETT, even if she hadn't picked me. Then Aunty Blaze said maybe I should try to talk to JETT about it, and everyone pretty much fell off their chair because Aunty Blaze is not usually one for chitchat, being more of an action-type person. And then she said, "WHAT? I can do chatchitting!" And we all laughed because she could barely even say it, let alone do it!

After dinner, when After Aunty Blaze and Uncle Titanooooooo had zoomed home, I went to my room to have a good think and to let my mouth cool down because Dad's CHiLi use was getting waaaay out of hand.

OBVIOUSLY I started to paint my nails, what with the thinking and having a new color to try out (*Witch's Hair*), and **OBVIOUSLY** as soon as I had finished the first hand, **WANDA** came in and told me that we had to go on a **special mission**,

and before I could even ask,
she said NO, there was no time
for my nails to dry. . . .

Why does the world always need saving
EVERY SINGLE TIME I start to paint
my nails (well, almost)? There are NEVER
any missions that need my urgent attention
when I am in the middle of a telling-off
from **Mum** or **Dad**, or when I have double
homework. **Typical.**

OUR HEROES ARRIVE IN BIG CITY...
...IT'S WORSE THAN THEY THOUGHT, BUT WHAT TO DO?

PING

SUDDENLY...
PIZAZZ HAS AN IDEA...

MOTHMAN CAN'T RESIST THE *LIGHT*...

OOOOH! THE LOVELY, LOVELY LIGHT...

NNNGGGHHH

NOW ALL PIZAZZ HAS TO DO IS KEEP HAVING IDEAS...

OOOOF

SPLAT

HHMMMTMFFF

OOOOF

...SO MOTHMAN KEEPS FLINGING HIMSELF AT THE *LOVELY, LOVELY LIGHT...OOOOF!*

HOORAY! OUR PLUCKY HERO KEPT HAVING IDEAS UNTIL MOTHMAN HAD QUITE EXHAUSTED HIMSELF AND WENT HOME TO LIE DOWN.

BIG CITY IS *SAVED!!!*

HMPH

THE NEXT MORNING...

What with staying up saving the world and smudging my nails the night before, I woke up late and my morning was all muddled.

FIRST...
CEREAL WITH JUICE ON IT

THEN...
BRUSHING HAIR WITH TOOTHBRUSH...

...*AND* BRUSHING TEETH WITH HAIRBRUSH

SHUT EYE ROLL

MEANWHILE...

UNDERPANTS ON HEAD

WHAT?

AND FINALLY...

PUTTING BACKPACK ON THE WRONG WAY

I was sooo groggy and late that **Dad** gave me and RED a lift to school, and as we got near, **Dad** did the really awful thing he always does and turned up the music in the car, which he thinks makes him a **supercool dad**, but obviously it doesn't because there is **NO SUCH THING. . . .**

WAYS DADS THINK THEY ARE COOL★... BUT REALLY AREN'T

DANCING...ERRRR, NO.

HEY! THOSE TRAINERS ARE WELL SICK!

TRYING TO BE DOWN WITH THE KIDZ... BLEURGH!

USING TOO MUCH HAIR STUFF...

...AND STILL HAVING BAD HAIR!

THINKING THEY'RE FASHIONABLE...

SOOOO NOT!

THINKING THEY ARE HILARIOUS.

100% NOT!!

EYE ROLL

EYE ROLL

73

Then, of course, **Dad** pulled up **RIGHT IN FRONT OF THE WHOLE SCHOOL**. This was bad enough, what with his "tunes" blaring out, but then he held his hand out for an actual high five like we were buddies or something. Then I got so flustered with the awfulness of it all that I managed to accidentally headbutt his hand. Like a high-face-five or something equally **COMPLETELY EMBARRASSING**.

And as I have the worst

luck in the world EVER, **Serena** was there with **The Populars** and **JETT**, and they all laughed so much their hair clips slipped. (Well, not **JETT'S**. **JETT** doesn't wear hair clips—why would she when she has sports hair? You know, the sort of hair that is perfect for sports, all swingy but not so swingy that it would get in your eyes, and no matter how much *whizzing* about you do, it just *swooshes* back into place.) And she wasn't exactly laughing quite so hard as **The Populars**, not quite.

As I walked to class, I saw **JETT** go into the bathroom on her own. Maybe this was the perfect moment to have that chatchit (HA HA) **Aunty Blaze** talked about. I couldn't go straight in with **SUPERS** having one another's backs and whatnot, that would be **TOO MUCH**, but maybe I could warn **JETT** about how **Serena** could actually be a bit mean, and let her know I would still be her friend if she wanted. I had to start somewhere, so I followed her inside.

I didn't want to look like a **cOMPLete weiRdo**, so I went up to the mirror and tried to think of a reason to be there, and all I could think of was lip balm. **Obviously** I didn't have any actual lip balm—I don't know what it is about lip balm, but it's like it just **WANTS** to get lost. Anyway, I did have an eraser that was the same shape as a lip balm (well, lip balm-ish). So I found that at the bottom of my bag and pretended to put it on.

JETT came over to the sinks to wash her hands, and I tried to smile, but I almost swallowed the eraser, so I gave up with the smiling and went straight into chat-chitting. I started with "Hello," a good solid start, but then suddenly my head emptied of **EVERYTHING** and I couldn't think of a single thing to say, so I offered **JETT** some of my lip balm, and when it was far too late, I remembered my lip balm was, in fact, an eraser. . . .

I was all ready for **JETT** to start laughing again and I could feel my cheeks going SUPER red, but she didn't. She just smiled and said no thanks, and not even in a sarcastic way, and I wondered if maybe, after all, we might be friends. Suddenly I thought of lots of things to say, like "Nice capelet" and "Isn't being **SUPER** a bit stinky sometimes?" but then **Serena** walked in with **The Populars** and asked **JETT** who she was talking to because all she could see was NOBODY, and **JETT** looked at the floor and I felt my cheeks go even redder, which I wasn't sure was possible but it turns out it was, and they all left the bathroom.

Then I wanted to be beamed up. Yes, even onto a **gunk-o-tron alien spaceship**, but there was no time for that because then the bell rang for attendance.

5

All morning Serena and The Populars and JETT were whispering and giggling and I felt all uncomfortable and hot, which was probably mostly down to my BRIGHT RED cheeks, but also because of feeling like a total nitwit and being a bit confused. JETT had almost been friendly, but as soon as Serena walked into the bathroom, that all seemed to change.

All I had wanted to do was be friendly. I REALLY tried to remember what Uncle Titanoooooo and Aunty Blaze had said, but now I felt far too embarrassed to want to be at all nice. UGH, why was everything so completely impossible?

After spending the whole morning practically itchy with embarrassment, I was worried I wouldn't be able to face lunch, but then I remembered it was pizza day. **HOORAY!** Finally, something to be happy about. As I walked through the cafeteria with **Ivy**, **Molly**, and **Ed** I felt even happier. I had three great friends. **AND PIZZA.**

In fact, everything was going brilliantly-ish, until I was walking back to our table and my stupid long, flappy cape got caught on one of **The Populars'** backpacks. **Of course**

it had to be one of **The Populars'** backpacks and **of course** it would happen right in the middle of the cafeteria and **of course** I went flying and **of course** my whole tray of milk, pizza, salad, yogurt, and cookies went

straight
        in
            my
                face.   **Of course.**

That would NEVER have happened if I had a capelet.

As I lay on the floor and felt the milk oozing through my hair, I blinked away the yogurt and thought about how things like this ALWAYS happen to me. I think it's because my balance is a bit stinky and has been ever since I was hit on the head by a **LLAMA**. (It's still a long story.) That and my completely and utterly useless FLAPPY CAPE.

Just then my thoughts were interrupted by **Serena's** spiky laugh,

HA! HA! HA!

followed by the laughs of **The Populars**,

HA! HA! HA! HA! HA!

and then . . . **JETT** laughed too.

Ivy helped me up, and **Ed** and **Molly** put everything (well, what was left of everything) back on my tray. And **Serena** leaned over to **JETT** and **LOUDLY** muttered (this is muttering but in a really obvious loud way that everyone is supposed to hear) that she was pleased there was at least *one* **SUPER** that was ACTUALLY **SUPER** in our class now. That really hurt, especially as I had saved the planet only hours before and she didn't even know it, and even if she did, I very much doubted she would have said thank you.

I turned around and said that actually, while I might not be brilliant at wearing a cape and carrying lunch at the same time, I was actually **SUPER** and was about to mention the world-saving the night before, but I didn't get to that bit because **Serena** started laughing a little bit like a donkey. NO ONE else in the whole school could get away with laughing like that without being teased. And then I realized why **Serena** could . . .

because she's the person who does all the teasing, and that made me even crosser. Then, before my brain had the chance to properly think it all through (darn that **LLAMA**!!), I just blurted out that I **WAS SUPER** . . . just as super as **JETT** . . . Maybe I was EVEN **SUPER**-ER. Suddenly the donkey-laughing stopped and an evil glint shone out of **Serena's** eyes, as evil as any baddie I have ever met. Right then I would rather have been anywhere else in the entire universe. Even in an enclosed space with **FARTERELLA**.

Serena looked at **JETT** and asked if she was going to let her (me) talk about her (**JETT**) like that. **JETT** stopped laughing and looked a bit uncomfortable. Then **Serena** asked again and the evil glint spread into her voice, and it felt like the whole cafeteria was holding their breath. **JETT** looked up just as a blob of yogurt dropped off the end of my nose, and she said she supposed not.

"Well," **Serena** said, far more loudly than she really needed to (DRAMA), "I guess that means we should have a

SUPER-OFF!!!

Apparently that way we would find out who actually is the MOST **SUPER SUPERHERO** in our class. And of course everyone seemed to agree with Serena that this was an **excellent idea**, because of course they would.

I lost my appetite after that, which was no bad thing as there wasn't much left on my lunch tray on account of me wearing most of it. Ivy came with me to the bathroom to help me mop the yogurty pizza and everything else off.

As we were mopping, I told Ivy I was really glad it wasn't a very hot day, because when old yogurt gets warm it smells like baby puke. (I *might* have accidentally left one on the radiator at home for a few days once.) Ivy laughed and said yes but we had PE later, so I was sure to stink after that, and I wondered why Ivy has to tell the complete and utter truth

THE WHOLE TIME.

I mean, it's not like I want her to lie, but maybe I don't need ALL the truth sometimes.

The bell rang and we ambled to class for the afternoon. (I didn't want to walk too quickly and overheat myself, yogurt-stink-wise.) Mrs. Harris was a bit late, and Serena used this time to make an announcement. I couldn't *wait* to hear what she had to say. . . . *

* I REALLY could.

Obviously **Serena** had put herself in charge of the **SUPER-OFF**, and I couldn't help but feel that this was pretty unfair as she was not even trying to hide who she absolutely wanted to win. (Clue: NOT ME.) But there was nothing I could do about it because it was out and all over school, and there was nothing else to do but to see it through to the end. Whatever the "end" was. **UGH.**

Serena marched up to the front of the class and one of **The Populars** called for quiet and everyone stopped talking waaaaay faster than they do for **Mrs. Harris**. Except for Karl Cuthbert, but he literally NEVER stops talking. Ever. Then **Serena** did a funny little cough and told everyone that there would be three **SUPER-OFF** contests, and whoever won the most would be the winner. Then she said everyone should come to watch the first **SUPER-OFF**, which would take place TODAY on the field at dismissal, and it would be . . .

Clap

I looked over at JETT, who looked back at me, and we both sort of shrugged like we didn't really care, but I knew I really did. And I thought JETT probably did too.

Then I felt very

STRONGLY

that **today** was

probably **not** going to

be **my day**....

6

The first SUPER-OFF bit . . .

The next lesson took **FOREVER** and also *FLEW BY* all at once, just like a mission I went on when I got stuck in a time vortex on the outer reaches of the **WONDER GALAXY**, trying to defeat the Time-a-nator.

It was **FRENCH**, and my tummy was making **REALLY** loud noises, so loud that at one point Mr. Petit (which is classic, because he is actually the tallest person EVER) thought I was asking a question. This made me wonder whether my tummy had a better **FRENCH** accent than me, and I thought the answer was probably *OUI*.

I wasn't actually sure whether it was rumbling because I had worn my lunch instead of eaten it OR because I was getting a bit worried about the **SUPER-OFF** after school. **Ivy** snuck me a cereal bar, and it was still noisy after that, so I reckoned it must be the worry.

It was bad enough that I had to do this stupid contest without ever even being asked if I really wanted to or not (I DID NOT), but having to do it AFTER SCHOOL was just too much. I started to tell **Ivy** it was **SO UNFAIR** that while **JETT** was technically the **NEW KID**, she was somehow already cooler and way more popular than me and—

Ivy put her hand on my shoulder and said that I really shouldn't worry. Sure, **JETT** had a more practical cape . . . sure, she had been befriended instantly by the most popular girls in school . . . and sure, she had

REALLY great sports hair, BUT she, **Molly**, and **Ed** would always be my friends and loyal **ECO COUNCIL** members (ahem, I was technically in charge, being *eco-monitor*) no matter what, and they thought I was **SUPER** in lots of ways. And then I was really glad that Ivy only ever told the truth. So glad I only did a tiny  EYE ROLL because, I mean, COME ON, my hair is **AWESOME** too. **Right?**

Finally, it was dismissal time and my cape was actually starting to smell like baby puke, which was making me feel sick too. So I wondered if I was actually just too sick to do the contest, and then I realized if I didn't do it today it would still be there tomorrow and that made me feel EVEN SICKER. BLEURGH!

Ivy, **Molly**, and **Ed** had come with me for moral support, which I really appreciated, as it seemed like the whole rest of the school was there too, and they all seemed to be supporting JETT.

I'm not sure why I thought that. . . .

Serena, The Populars, and JETT were nowhere to be seen, which I thought was extremely rude as it was all their idea in the first place. Then I wondered if it had all just been a joke, or maybe JETT had sprained her ankle and couldn't make it, and I was just starting to feel a bit more normal when I saw them all walk around the corner of the science block, and my tummy dropped down to my toes.

Everyone went quiet, and Serena declared the first **SUPER-OFF** would be a *COMIC STRIP BATTLE*. . . .

FLYING SPECTACULAR

PIZAZZ VS. JETT...

YOUR FIRST SUPER-OFF CHALLENGE IS THE, LIKE, *FLYING SPECTACULAR*...OKAY? I, LIKE, WANT TO SEE WHO IS THE BEST AT, LIKE, FLYING. SO I WANT YOU BOTH TO, LIKE, DO SOME FLYING STUNTS AND STUFF, YEAH? AND THEN WHOEVER, LIKE, DOES THEM BEST WILL BE THE ACTUAL WINNER...*HUH?*

SO YOUR FIRST CHALLENGE, IS, LIKE, A LOOP THE LOOP...

READY... SET... **GO!**

OH, COME ON...

AND THEN IT BECAME CLEAR WHY JETT WAS CALLED, ER, JETT...

UNSURPRISINGLY JETT WINS THE FIRST, LIKE, CHALLENGE. THE SECOND CHALLENGE IS TO, LIKE, GO TO THE, LIKE, MOON AND, LIKE, BACK...

LIKE, I, LIKE, HAVE A CHOICE!

READY...SET... *GOOOOOO!*

EEEK!

ZOOM!

HA HA HA

JETT MAKES IT BACK IN NO TIME AT ALL... BUT WHERE'S PIZAZZ?...

HMMMMMM...

YAWN

THUMP!

AND JETT, LIKE, TOTALLY WINS THAT CHALLENGE TOO. NEXT I, LIKE, WANT YOU TO, LIKE, WRITE YOUR, LIKE, NAME IN THE, LIKE, SKY.

WELL, THAT SEEMS FAIR AS MY NAME IS *MILES* LONGER THAN JETT'S!

A GOOD START FOR PIZAZZ...

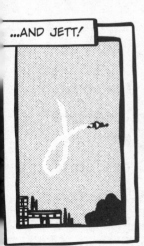

...AND JETT!

ZOOOOOOM

WHIZZZZZZ

UH-OH!...

OH NO!!! DISASTER!!! PIZAZZ HAS GOTTEN TANGLED IN HER CAPE AND...

OH DEAR...JETT 3–PIZAZZ 0

CRASH!

THUDDDDDDD!!!

PERFECT LANDING!

I didn't think it needed saying at this point, but even so, Serena stood on the wall outside the science block and announced JETT was the winner. JETT looked happy as everyone cheered (yes, even me, Ivy, **Molly**, and **Ed**, because you have to be a good sport no matter what), and I didn't blame her. I think I would have been happy and pleased if I had won, so I couldn't be cross with JETT. I did wonder whether the lap of honor and high-fiving everyone as she *ran* past them was a

bit much. When she did a backflip, then the robot, and then a knee *skid*, I thought that was just getting to be a bit **showy-offy**.

But it was when **JETT** looked over at me with my stupid long cape in a knot, covered in lunch, smelling like baby puke, and she laughed along with the others, that's when it felt the most horrible, and I wondered if maybe she had gone to

THE DARK SIDE.

So much for **SUPERS** having each other's backs.

After school, **Ivy** walked home with me and tried to cheer me up. This was really nice of her, but what with my total **SUPER-OFF** defeat, PE/yogurt stink, and **Ivy** only being able to tell the absolute truth, it was a bit too much of a challenge, so we mainly walked in silence. But that was okay.

When we got to my house, I was about to ask if she wanted to come over for dinner, when **WANDA** trotted over, blurting out a mission. Of course she couldn't have done that after school to save me from complete embarrassment in front of **EVERYONE,**

OH NO!

LISTEN UP, SUPERS: THE SUPER-SNEAKY, EVER-SO-BEAKY BADDIE, NOSTRILAMOUS, IS BACK AT WORK SNIFFING OUT VERY FAMOUS AND EXTREMELY EXPENSIVE STUFF. HE HAS JUST SNIFFED OUT SOME UTTERLY PRICELESS WORKS OF ART THAT ARE *VERY IMPORTANT.* YOU MUST STOP HIM FROM STEALING THEM AND RUINING *EVERYTHING....*

NOSTRILAMOUS

OH NO!

SNIFF SNIFF SNIFF

THOSE DOUBLE-IMPORTANT WORKS OF ART ARE AS GOOD AS *GONE....*

BUT WAIT!

...OUR HEROES ARE ZOOMING IN!

ZOOOOM

HOORAY! THEY ARE CLOSING IN...

WHIFF

SNIFF SNIFF SNIFF

HANG ON! *NOSTRILAMOUS,* WHAT'S THAT **DISGUSTING** SMELL?

PHEW! OUR HEROES HAVE ARRIVED AT THE SCENE OF THE CRIME, WELL, CRIME TO BE...

EEEEUUUUUUUUUUWWWWWWW!!!!! THAT DISGUSTING SMELL IS GETTING STRONGER...

ARGH! STAY BACK, YOU STINKER!

SMELLIANT!!!!!

NOSTRILAMOUS'S SUPER-SENSITIVE NOSTRILS HAVE BEEN UTTERLY BLASTED BY THE HORRIBLE YOGURTY STINK OF OUR SMELLY SUPERHERO, LEAVING HIM UTTERLY POWERLESS, AND THE PRICELESS WHATNOT IS SAFE AND SOUND.

STINK POWER!!!!!

When we got back, **Dad** asked why on earth I was still wearing my **STINKY** cape and why wasn't I in the bath? I wanted to say because **first** of all, I had to take part in a stupid **SUPER-OFF**, during which I got to be **humiliated** in front of the whole school, then **secondly** I had to go and save the world as soon as I got home with no time for even a tiny snack, and then **thirdly**, I was **busy having a lecture** about **STINKY** capes!

But I didn't because I was **too tired**.

So I just went and ran a bath.

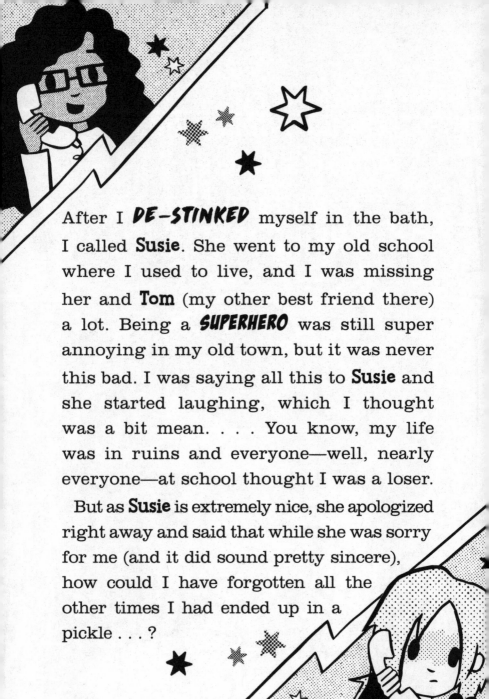

After I **DE-STINKED** myself in the bath, I called **Susie**. She went to my old school where I used to live, and I was missing her and **Tom** (my other best friend there) a lot. Being a **SUPERHERO** was still super annoying in my old town, but it was never this bad. I was saying all this to **Susie** and she started laughing, which I thought was a bit mean. . . . You know, my life was in ruins and everyone—well, nearly everyone—at school thought I was a loser.

But as **Susie** is extremely nice, she apologized right away and said that while she was sorry for me (and it did sound pretty sincere), how could I have forgotten all the other times I had ended up in a pickle . . . ?

I said that I guess that was JUST MY LUCK and all *that* proved was that I was **DOOMED** wherever I lived, and then **Susie** started laughing again. REALLY? But then she reminded me of all the times she had gotten into a pickle herself, and **Tom**, too, and even one time **RED** did.

I was thrilled she had reminded me about THAT, because I had forgotten all about it, and now I could "mention" it the next time **RED** went from being just **extremely annoying** to **extra extremely annoying**.

WHEN RED *ACCIDENTALLY* CALLED THE TEACHER "MUM"...

MUM

WHEN TOM *ACCIDENTALLY* WORE HIS SLIPPERS TO SCHOOL...

HA! HA! HA! HA! HA! HA!

WHEN SUSIE FORGOT SHE WAS ON THE BUS AND STARTED SINGING...

LA LA LAA

SHUUUUT UP!!

THEN . . .

Susie pointed out that we all had our moments. There were **Serenas everywhere**, and there wasn't much we could do about that. But what we could do was decide how we *reacted* to the **Serenas**. And then I remembered why **Susie** was one of my absolute best friends ever—her excellent advice. That, and how we both love marzipan when almost no one else seems to.

Then we talked about her school show (she's in charge of lighting and **Tom** is painting scenery), how unfair homework is, how annoying little sisters are (she has one too). Then **RED** came in and told me it was lights out, like the complete **goody-goody** she always is. I was ignoring her very successfully, and then **Mum** yelled up the stairs that I had to listen to my sister. It's all wrong—I am the BIG sister here, so how come she gets to do the bossing about?

Susie said she had to go too, and wished me luck for the rest of the **SUPER-OFF**, but also pointed out that I shouldn't worry about it too much because it would all be ancient history in a couple of weeks, and I sort of agreed. Then I hung up and tried to get to sleep. . . .

I WOKE UP because I smelled the most **DISGUSTING** smell in the whole world (and I have smelled one of DABOMB'S SUPER-STINKY STINK BOMBS AND **Dad's** socks). It turned out to be **WANDA'S** breath. And the reason I could smell **WANDA'S** breath was because she was standing on my chest, licking my face! Apparently,

this was to wake me up because—joy of joys—we had a mission to go on . . . **BEFORE BREAKFAST**.

I saw that **Mum** had put out a new cape for me, and I hoped this one actually fit, but no. There was still plenty of room for me to grow into it.*

*TRIP OVER IT.

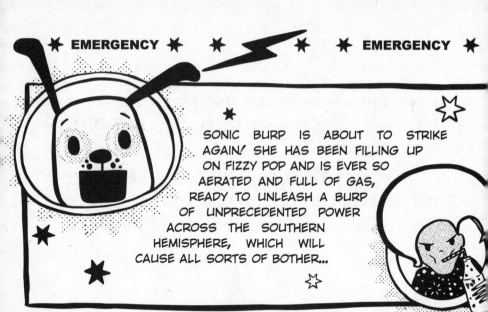

SONIC BURP IS ABOUT TO STRIKE AGAIN! SHE HAS BEEN FILLING UP ON FIZZY POP AND IS EVER SO AERATED AND FULL OF GAS, READY TO UNLEASH A BURP OF UNPRECEDENTED POWER ACROSS THE SOUTHERN HEMISPHERE, WHICH WILL CAUSE ALL SORTS OF BOTHER...

HERE COME THE GIRLS... WELL, AND THEIR MUM...

VVVOO OOOP

OUR SUPERHEROES LOCATE SONIC BURP IN DOUBLE-QUICK TIME AND FIND HER GULPING DOWN SOME EXTRA AIR...

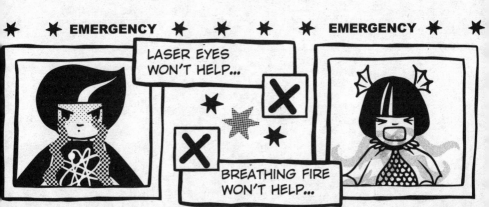

LASER EYES WON'T HELP...

BREATHING FIRE WON'T HELP...

THERE'S ONLY ONE THING TO DO...

...OUR BRAVE AND EXTREMELY EMBARRASSED HERO TAKES HER PLACE AND WAITS FOR JUST THE RIGHT MOMENT...

GURGLE

GULP

A SPLIT SECOND BEFORE THE BURP ERUPTS, PIZAZZ CREATES A GLITTER STORM THAT GOES RIGHT UP SONIC BURP'S NOSE, MAKING HER SNIFF THE BURP BACK DOWN. WHERE WILL IT END UP? WELL, I THINK THE LESS SAID ABOUT THAT THE BETTER...BUT EMERGENCY AVERTED!

FOR NOW!

On the way home, **Dad** told me that he'd bumped into the new **SUPERS** in the supermarket—no, that's not a market for **SUPERHEROES**, it's just a normal supermarket where you buy food and stuff. **Dad** said they seemed really nice and so he'd invited them all over for dinner tonight. I asked him if he meant *all* of them and not just the grown-up ones, and he said yes, and I said "great" in a way I really hoped let everyone know just how **NOT GREAT** I actually thought it was. Then I

zoomed

ahead of everyone else because . . . **UGH**.

GRUMBLE

FURIOUS CHOCO POPS

GRUMBLE!

By the time everyone got home I was halfway through my second bowl of **FURIOUS CHOCO POPS**. The **CHOCO POPS** themselves weren't furious, but I was. I mean, **REALLY**? It just felt like everyone was on Team **JETT**—Serena, The Populars, the rest of the WHOLE school (minus Ivy, **Molly**, **Ed**, and possibly RED)—and now my parents had invited her for **DINNER**!

EYE ROLL

It felt super unfair that I had been here the *whole* time (well, since **Mum** and **Dad** made us move here), trying my best (ish) to be the **SUPER** that I am supposed to be, then **JETT** comes along and right away, without her even trying, everyone thinks she's amazing. I really tried to remember what **Susie** had told me on the phone the night before, I really did, but when your own actual parents aren't on your side, it's just **TOO** much. Then I remembered I hadn't actually told my own parents what was going on, but shouldn't they have guessed or even sensed it? I mean, one of them has mind reading as a bonus **SUPERPOWER**, for goodness's sake.

As they walked through the door, I guessed that **RED** had told **Mum** and **Dad** *everything* because they were looking at me in that funny way parents do when they are trying to be nice but usually looks a bit creepy. **Mum** said that having the other **SUPER** family (including **JETT**) over might actually be a good thing, and I wondered if she had been hit on the head by a **LLAMA** too (that **LLAMA** has **A LOT** to answer for). She said if I gave **JETT** a chance she might actually turn out to be nice, and we might even end up being really good friends because we had so much in common.

Then I asked her why, for someone who could read minds (a side effect of having *LASER EYES*, apparently), she managed to have

ABSOLUTELY NO CLUE ABOUT MY LIFE WHATSOEVER.

She replied, saying something about respecting my privacy (er, maybe try knocking before you barge into my room, then) and not knowing what she might find in there **(charming)**.

Despite my very best efforts (which were *not* helped by RED singing along to her favorite annoying boy band the whole way there), I was even crosser by the time I arrived at school. I just wanted to get this stupid **SUPER-OFF** over with, then things could get back to normal. I would be a super loser, and Serena and JETT would still be super popular and that would be FINE.

When I got into the classroom, I was just in time to hear Serena announce that the next **SUPER-OFF** would be at lunchtime on the sports field. **GREAT.**

Every single lesson that morning seemed to go on forever, and I really couldn't concentrate on anything much, as I was trying to work out how on Earth (or in outer space) I would be completely humiliated this time. I tried to talk about it with Ivy in physics because we were lab partners, but I got told off by Miss Walker, who said we really should actually pay attention as we didn't want another repeat of "the egg experiment incident." And she was right—we really didn't . . . but that wasn't only my fault, the laws of physics were also to blame.

THE EGG
(BEFORE THE
EXPERIMENT INCIDENT)

BUT we did manage to discuss it during drama. Well, we mime-discussed it because it was a mime class . . . and it turns out that **SUPER—OFFS** are actually pretty hilarious when you mime them. . . .

THE BIT WHERE SERENA
ANNOUNCES THE
SUPER-OFF

THE FLYING BIT

I was just starting to feel a bit better about everything (because it is an actual scientific fact that giggling always helps), when I made the massive mistake of looking at the clock. It was five minutes to lunchtime and my stomach flipped, and while I really tried to be all cool and calm, I mainly wasn't.

After we had a quick lunch, **Ivy**, **Molly**, **Ed**, and I walked to the sports field. It really did help that they were there (I would have been double nervous on my own), but I knew that very soon it would all come down to me, and no matter how many times I told myself . . .

. . . it still felt like it was a **really big** thing. And when I thought about it like that, I got a little bit cross again, but this time with myself.

WOW! PIZAZZ HAS BADDIE OPTIONS!...SHOULD SHE CATCH AUNTY FURY OR KAPOW? HMMM, BUT THERE WAS THAT HULLABALOO AUNTY FURY CAUSED LAST CHRISTMAS, KAPOW IT IS! UNFORTUNATELY, JETT DOESN'T HAVE QUITE SO MANY OPTIONS. IN FACT, SHE HAS NO ACTUAL OPTIONS....

WOOOOOOO! and HOOOOOOOOOOO!

I won. I couldn't believe it, but I won! I guess I was a **SUPER** super after all! Well, a super who happened to have a **super-secret**, super-baddie best friend. Whatever . . . **I WON!**

Maybe I WAS just as super as **JETT**? Maybe I was actually even **SUPERER?!**

It was 1–1 in the **SUPER-OFF**, with one more contest to go, which meant I could actually win the whole thing and be the **WINNER!**

Ivy, **Molly**, and **Ed** came over to congratulate me! Yes, ME! The **WINNER!** I turned around and saw **JETT** trailing after **Serena**, who was **storming** off with her nose in the air, and although I knew deep down it probably shouldn't, it actually did make me feel a bit good. See how they like it for a change!

I looked around me, and **Ivy**, **Molly**, and **Ed** were looking at me like I had three heads and all those heads had **Mrs. Wiggin's** (the scariest lunch lady ever, and she has some tough competition) face on them, and then I realized I had been thinking out loud.

Ivy told me, **VERY** seriously, to remember the **SUPER-OFF** didn't actually mean anything, and as I of all people knew what Serena was really like, I should realize JETT was probably a nice person, but she was just being bossed around by Serena. As Ivy said all this, I knew she was probably right, but the problem was . . . I sort of wasn't listening. . . .

The bit where Jett comes over for dinner . . .

154

The rest of the day *flew* by, which was annoying as I was quite enjoying people smiling at me and congratulating me on winning the second **SUPER-OFF** contest. I quite liked being a winner, and while I felt a little bit bad for **JETT**, someone had to be the loser. Didn't they?

I even started to think about doing some training after school for the final **SUPER-OFF** contest the next day. Then I stopped thinking about that and decided to paint my nails. (I had a new shade to try out—**DEAD BEETLE**.) They would be my lucky nails!

As soon as I got home, I suddenly remembered **JETT'S SUPER** family were coming over for dinner!

Why tonight? I had *far* more important things to be doing, like getting in the ZONE, digging deep, putting my eyes on the PRIZE (oh, what if there was an actual prize?), and of course painting my lucky nails. But then I wondered if I could get any useful information out of **JETT'S** parents. If I was super sneaky, they might accidentally tell me **JETT'S** weaknesses. Maybe she was scared of something . . . *spiders? Cotton balls? Long words?* (Which is called Hippopotomonstrosesquippedaliophobia. **REALLY??**)

OOOOOOH,

maybe she's terrified of clowns?

As I dragged my backpack through the kitchen on my way to my room, **Mum** told me **JETT** and her family were coming over in an hour so to get all my homework done and to wash my face and hands and try to think of this as an opportunity to make a new friend.

PUH-LEASE! I smiled what I thought was my **winningest** I-have-listened-to-everything-you-have-said-so-will-you-please-stop-talking-to-me-now smile at **Mum**, but

she just told me not to be sarcastic. So she was reading my mind after all.

I really did try to do my homework, but I couldn't concentrate because my brain only seemed to be able to imagine me winning the whole **SUPER-OFF** the next day and all the wonderful things that would happen as a result of me being the **SUPER CHAMPION**! It was pretty great . . . but then the doorbell rang and ruined EVERYTHING.

By the time I'd gotten downstairs, **WANDA** was licking **JETT'S** hand and **RED** was telling her to think about joining the student council volunteer squad, which obviously **RED** is in charge of. How could they side with the enemy like this? **TRAITORS!!!** Unfortunately, I accidentally said that last part out loud (I need to stop doing that), which made things a bit **MORE** awkward. I wasn't sure what to do next, so I just looked over at **JETT** with a look that I really hope said, "Yeah, whatever, you can have my dog and my annoying little sister, that's fine by me." I'm not sure it actually did say that,

though, because **JETT** just looked a bit confused. So I decided to go with my original plan and try to dig up some dirt on **JETT** by talking to her parents. . . .

Unfortunately, after a good twenty minutes of small talk, I only managed to accidentally let them know I was afraid of **JELL-O**, which was not the plan at all, but I didn't see how that would help **JETT** tomorrow. And I had managed not to mention it was specifically

orange JELL-O.
HAH!

JETT'S parents actually seemed surprisingly nice, and **BILLY-BOB**, their pet terrier, who is basically their version of **WANDA**, was also nice. All that made me wonder if **JETT** might actually be nice after all. . . . Well, when she wasn't hanging out with **Serena**, that is. But then I quickly stopped because that sort of thinking was not going help me be **ULTIMATE AND SUPREME CHAMPION** tomorrow. . . . .

Not. At. ALL.

Dinner was double awkward, especially because **Mum** put **JETT** and me opposite each other so we "could talk," and we did, but just with our eyes, and I am almost positive all our eyes were saying, "I will beat you tomorrow, just you wait." I even accidentally ate some mushrooms because my eyes were so busy telling **JETT** she was going to lose tomorrow, they forgot to check what I was eating. I tried not to let this show on my face, but I am fairly certain that is impossible.

After saying almost nothing for **two hours** (except with my eyes, obvs), it was finally time to say to goodbye (with my mouth) to **JETT** and her surprisingly nice family. They had to leave early as **BILLY-BOB** blurted out a mission for them halfway through dessert, and I have never been happier that the world was in certain peril.

Just as they all headed for the door, **JETT** whispered that she was glad **Mission Control** had picked the right **SUPER** for the job and not a nitwit who couldn't even carry their lunch on a tray. So obviously I did the responsible and mature thing . . . and stuck my tongue out at her.

Of course, no one else heard **JETT**, but **Mum** saw me stick my tongue out and decided to make a big old fuss over it. She even wanted me apologize when **I HADN'T EVEN STARTED IT**! And what made it all the more annoying was seeing **JETT** smirk while I was getting told off!

So obviously I got sent to my room.

I picked up **BERNARD** on the way. I thought I would fill her in on what had happened since I last spoke to her—she might have some brilliant advice, or just want to eat my schoolbooks again. Anyway, while I was telling her all about it and how it was SO **COMPLETELY** UNFAIR and how even my own family were on **JETT'S** side, I could have sworn I heard some eyes rolling. I *whizzed* around, and sure enough, there was **KAPOW**, and he wasn't just eye rolling, he was laughing as well. Rude.

When he finally stopped laughing, **KAPOW** said that no matter what happened at the **SUPER-OFF**, **Serena** would still think I'm a loser, because she is mean like that. But that even though I can be annoying and drag him into silly **SUPER-OFFS** that he REALLY didn't want to be part of, and even talk to guinea pigs, HE didn't think I was a loser. And I didn't have to, either.

KAPOW pointed out that **JETT** and I would always be supers (whether we wanted to be or not) and we will both carry on saving the world no matter who wins or who loses. As far as **KAPOW** could tell, **Serena** seemed to be one of those people who just likes causing lots of fuss and by being all huffy and grumpy and moan-y, all I was doing was helping her. . . . And why was I being so silly and letting her turn being **SUPER** into a stupid competition?

Silly? Err, I think you mean **WINNER**. I was FINALLY just about to actually WIN something and **KAPOW** calls it STUPID?

THANKS! Well, I'd show him silly AND stupid and I told him so too. . . . I couldn't believe that even my longest, most **secret**, and best friend didn't understand. He'd obviously never been a NOBODY at school, but this was my chance to be liked—yes, maybe even be POPULAR— and I wasn't going to let him ruin it.

KAPOW *zoomed off* and I was so fidgety from it all I gave BERNARD a tiny Mohawk, which actually looked awesome, and I realized my guinea pig might actually have better hair than me.

Then I went to bed. Tomorrow was going to be a big day.

9

The bit where I WIN ...
maybe ...

All the way to school the next morning, **R Ɛ D** went on and on about how the **SUPER-OFF** was nonsense and she really didn't get why **JETT** and I were letting **Serena** make us compete and blah blah **BLAAAAH**. Well, of course **R Ɛ D** didn't get it—she was super great at EVERYTHING without even trying. I just wanted to be great at this.

As **R Ɛ D** and I walked up the path to school, I suddenly realized everyone was smiling at ME! Saying hello to ME! Even wishing ME luck for later. **Wow!** This must be what it felt

like to be popular. . . . **R**ⅇ**D** rolled her eyes and I pointed out that she is categorically **NOT** allowed to roll her eyes as that is MY thing, and I was about to tell her that I have to give permission to anyone wanting to do it and I DO **NOT** GIVE HER PERMISSION, but then Jenny McGrath smiled at me, and she never smiles at **ANYONE**. Then I thought about how I liked everyone smiling at me and I decided I wanted more. **I had to win**. . . .

When I got into the classroom, Ivy was already there but looking a bit worried, again, so I told her she shouldn't worry because I was going to win today and school coolness would at last be MINE!

Then Ivy said, "Of course" in a way that suggested while that *might* happen it probably wouldn't. Then she said she was actually worried about JETT. So I asked her why, because, err, really? Being MY friend and everything, she should actually be worried about ME.

Ivy told me that Serena had been nagging JETT all morning about how she only hung out with winners and that JETT had better be a winner too.

Beautiful
Baby winner

Cutest Cupcake
winner

I reminded **Ivy** of all the times **Serena** had been mean to me (this took quite a while), and now it was my chance to show her and everyone else that I wasn't a total loser, and that MAYBE my friends could be a bit more supportive instead of worrying about the ENEMY.

Ivy pointed out that at least I had friends—apart from **Serena** and **The Populars**, **JETT** had no one, so I HAD to point out that ACTUALLY **JETT** had chosen **Serena** to be her friend, so . . .

Then I accidentally looked over at **JETT**, who was slumped down in her chair, and even her sports hair looked less swishy than normal. I accidentally felt bad for her, but then I remembered I had some **WINNING** to do and couldn't be worrying about that now.

At lunchtime **Serena** announced the final **SUPER-OFF** was during last period, and unsurprisingly, everyone thought that was a marvelous idea. Again.

I was a bit nervous about the final contest, so nervous I wasn't sure I would be able to manage any lunch, so I only had 1½ baked potatoes, beans, coleslaw, broccoli, a yogurt, some milk, an apple, and two pancakes. Once I'd gotten lunch out of the way, I decided to try out some tactics, and stared really hard

at **JETT**, so hard I was almost surprised actual *LASERS* didn't come out of my eyes.

Ivy and **Molly** noticed (**Ed** didn't as he was too interested in his giant cookie) and asked what I was doing. I said, wasn't it obvious? I was clearly psyching out my opponent.

Ivy asked why I was being so weird and what happened to me wanting to be **JETT'S** buddy?

EYE ROLL

Er, where had she been for the last two days? What was wrong with everyone?

I was just stomping out of the school hall when **JETT** got up and blocked my path, and I wobbled a bit because I had no idea what I was supposed to do. I tried to look taller than normal and a bit mean yet also unbothered all at the same time, but it was really hard and I don't think I managed it. So then I tried to walk around **JETT**, who just stepped to the side and blocked my path. I tried again and she just stepped the other way, and then she reached behind her and brought out **JELL-O**! Then **JETT** announced to the WHOLE school (well, the bit that was in the cafeteria) that I was *scared of* **JELL-O**. Well ha-ha-de-ha-ha, **JETT**, because that is a *strawberry* **JELL-O** and I am only afraid of—**ARGH!** Right then, **JETT** produced an ORANGE **JELL-O** from behind her back and there was nothing to do but to run out of the hall, maybe slightly screaming.

I don't know what it is . . . the glowing orangey wobbliness . . . it's . . . it's just *DISGUSTING*.

Ivy and **Molly** found me in the bathroom. I told them that after what had just happened, **I HAD TO WIN** or I would be even more of a loser than ever.

Ivy said I didn't need to win **Serena's** silly competition to prove anything, and I pointed out that how would she know, she didn't know what it was like to be a **SUPER**, with people expecting you to be, well, *super* all the time,

and **Serena** wasn't horrible to her and she didn't have to wear a stupid long cape **THE**

WHOLE

TIME.

NO ONE understood, **NO ONE** *got it*, and could **EVERYONE** just go away and leave me on my own. **NOW** . . . **PLEASE?**

Ivy and **Molly** looked a bit shocked, and I had a feeling I probably did too. I didn't like this feeling at all. And I didn't really want to be on my own, but it was too late now, I'd said it. Ivy and **Molly** walked out.

The afternoon went on forever and I couldn't even giggle with Ivy in study hall, what with us not speaking and everything, then finally the bell for afternoon break rang. This time I had to make the LOOOOONG walk up to the field on my own. It felt much more scary than when my friends had been with me, but I couldn't let anyone see that. . . . I had winning to do.

Serena, The Populars, and **JETT** (who was acting a bit like she was already the winner) were all standing on the wall. When they saw me, **Serena** nudged **JETT** and they wobbled around a bit, I guess like **JELL-O**. **Fun-ny.**

Serena summoned me up onto the wall and started to make a speech about how it was all her idea and now we would find out who really was the *SUPEREST SUPER* of them all, and the final contest

EYE ROLL

EYE ROLL

would be a race to bring back one of the rings of Saturn, and then I *eye rolled*. Even *I* know they aren't ACTUAL rings. They're just made up of millions of bits of space rock, moon pieces, and dust and stuff. I looked across at **JETT**, who looked a bit confused, like she had just thought the same thing. Then I looked at **Ivy**, who *eye rolled*. So did **Ed** and **Molly** (it really is catching on), then I saw **RED** do it too (which I surprisingly didn't mind right then) and suddenly I got a telepathic signal that even **KAPOW** was *eye rolling* and then I laughed out loud, because, well, it was all so **SILLY!**

Serena *really* didn't appreciate me laughing halfway through her dramatic **SUPER-OFF** final introduction. You could tell because her face went actual purple, and she just opened and closed her mouth a bit like a goldfish or PufferBoy (as in the fish, not the padded coat). Then I remembered what **Susie** and **KAPOW** (and possibly **BERNARD**) had said about how the

Serenas of this world (and possibly alien worlds too) can only be hurtful if we let them. I decided right then to take back **MY** power and do the thing that **SUPERHEROES** are trained to do from birth. . . .

I MONOLOGUED.

POSSIBLY A LONG TIME AGO IN

. . . but mainly this week, here at school dark forces have gathered and they only went and created the **SUPER-OFF**. Like absolute twits, **JETT** and I fell for it and have been running around trying to prove we are each more **SUPER** and generally better than the other. But in all that chaos we forgot **SUPERHERO** rule number one . . . that everyone has DIFFERENT superpowers, and instead of using them against each other, we should combine them to make the superest powers of all, like friendship, kindness, and jet-propelled glitter storms.

A GALAXY FAR, FAR AWAY . . .

We must always remember that while these dark forces can TRY to make us feel not at all super, we all have the power to decide how we react to them . . . maybe ignore them or maybe talk it over with some good forces or maybe just remind yourself that you are most definitely the superest you. EVER.

Oh yes, and you won't believe it, but the true meaning of life is . . .

BUT THEN . . .

Like so many good superhero monologues, it was interrupted by a baddie. . . . **Serena** stopped gaping her mouth and gained the power of speech, or should I say *screech*, and yelled, "GO!" at the top of her lungs. BUT at the exact same time, **WANDA** and **BILLY-BOB** appeared with an actual real Earth-saving mission for me and **JETT**! With **Serena** yelling and **WANDA** and **BILLY-BOB** blurting out our **mission**, it all got rather confusing. I looked at **JETT**, who looked at me, and we both knew exactly what to do . .

Ha-HA! Only joking, of course we went off to save the world. . . . And as we left Earth's atmosphere we could still hear *Serena* screeching. . . .

TWO-PLAYER COMBO...HOORAY
FOR THE JET-PROPELLED GLITTER STORM.
THE CANNONBALL IS *DEFEATED!*

10

The end bit . . .

Yes.

We saved the world,

again.

Because that's what **SUPERPOWERS** are really for, only sometimes we get it all a bit muddled.

By the time we got back to school, news of our actual **world-saving** had reached everyone, which I cannot help but feel had something to do with RED. I know she is honestly the most irritating little sister ever, but there are times when I am very glad she is *my* irritating little sister. She gave me the double thumbs-up, so I ***eye rolled*** and everything felt right again.

Everyone seemed **very excited** about what JETT and I had done. Well, everyone except Serena and The Populars. Well, Popular 1 looked excited until Serena jabbed her in the ribs, and then she just looked a bit in pain. JETT, and I were even given three cheers which Verity Bennett from the athletics team started. I had never had a three cheers before, and the one for luck really did take me by surprise.

Who knows, maybe by just being myself I might be *somebody* at school, maybe even a **bit popular**, maybe even a **bit cool**. I mean, I have the right hair for it. . . .

HIP HIP HOORAY

SCHOOL ✕ TIMES

WORLD SAVED

And all before the bell!!!

Me sneezing on my own glitter storm

Oh well, maybe not. But then, really, **who cares?**

JETT and I did become actual friends, and other than **Mum** constantly reminding me that she was right after all, I was very pleased about that. **Mission Control** even sends us on missions together sometimes. **JETT** politely declined our offer to join the **ECO COUNCIL**, but joined the athletics team instead. I mean, she has the perfect hair for it, so it made sense.

And I realized that my friends had been right the whole time. *I* had been giving **Serena** the power to upset me all along, and now it was time to take it away from her.

And I didn't even need to use my **jazz hands/glitter storm/** most embarrassing ***SUPER***POWER **EVER** to do it.

Result.

VERITY
ATHLETICS CAPTAIN

IVY
ECO COUNCIL

JAMIE
SPELLING BEE CHAMP

MOLLY
ECO COUNCIL

SARAH
STUDENT COUNCIL

SERENA
SCHOOL PRINCESS

POPULAR 1
CUTEST CUPCAKE

FREDDIE
YOGURT FAN CLUB

RED
GOOD AT EVERYTHING

JETT
100M CHAMPION

ED
ECO COUNCIL

JESSICA
LIBRARY AIDE

RICKY
HALL MONITOR

PIZAZZ
ECO COUNCIL

SUSAN
GYMNASTICS TEAM

SAFFRON
CHOIR CAPTAIN

POPULAR 2
BEAUTIFUL BABY

MRS. WIGGIN
LUNCH LADY OF DOOM

Don't miss Pizazz's first *SUPER* adventure,

and look out for